W9-AAO-956

Based on an experience told by Gladys Henton

Text © 1968 by Polly Greenberg
Revised text © 2002 by Polly Greenberg
Illustrations © 1968 by Aliki Brandenberg

First published in 1968 by Macmillan Publishing Co., Inc., New York.

All rights reserved. No part of this book may be reproduced or utilized in any form or by any means, electronic or mechanical, including photocopying, recording, or any information storage and retrieval system, without permission in writing from the publisher.

SEASTAR BOOKS
A division of NORTH-SOUTH BOOKS INC.

Published in 2002 in the United States by SeaStar Books, a division of North-South Books Inc., New York. Published simultaneously in Great Britain, Canada, Australia, and New Zealand by North-South Books, an imprint of Nord-Süd Verlag AG, Gossau Zürich, Switzerland.

Library of Congress Cataloging-in-Publication Data is available.
A CIP catalogue record for this book is available from The British Library.

ISBN 1-58717-122-8 (trade edition)
10 9 8 7 6 5 4 3 2 1 HC
ISBN 1-58717-123-6 (library edition)
10 9 8 7 6 5 4 3 2 1 LE

Printed in Hong Kong

For more information about our books, and the authors and artists who create them, visit our web site: www.northsouth.com

To children all over the world
who work hard to help their families.

When I was a little girl,
we walked out to the cotton field
early in the morning
with the sun shining pretty on the land.

My Daddy told us
if we picked a lot of cotton
we might get a sucker.

We picked and we picked
and we picked and we picked.

It was hot, oh my, it was hot.
I looked up with the water running
off my face,
and I saw a dog lying under a bush,
going huh-huh-huh like dogs do.

I said, "Oh Lord, I wish I was a dog."

We picked and we picked
and we picked and we picked.

It was hot, oh my, it was hot.
I looked up with the water running
off my face,
and I saw a buzzard, going round and round
and round in the sky like buzzards do.

I said, "Oh Lord, I wish I was a buzzard."

We picked and we picked
and we picked and we picked.

It was hot, oh my, it was hot.
I looked up with the water running
off my face,
and I saw a snake, curved up cold and
cool near a rock like snakes do.

I said, "Oh Lord, I wish I was a snake."

We picked and we picked
and we picked and we picked.

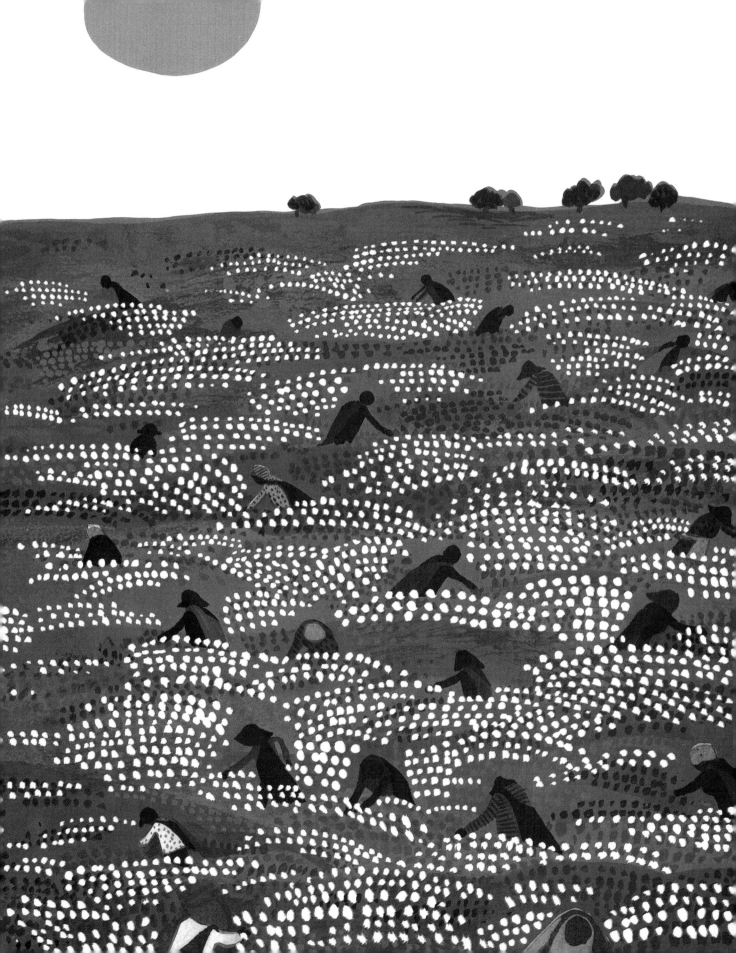

It was hot, oh my, it was hot.
I looked up with the water running
off my face,
and I saw a butterfly, bouncing from blossom
to blossom like butterflies do.

I said, "Oh Lord, I wish I was a butterfly."

We picked and we picked
and we picked and we picked.

It was hot, oh my, it was hot.
I looked up with the water running
off my face,
and I saw a partridge, circling
and clattering like partridges do.

I said, "Oh Lord, I wish I was a partridge."

When we were finished, on Saturday,
our Daddy gave us our suckers.
Mine was red.

I put the candy in my hand and the
stick in my mouth so all the kids
could see we had candy, lots of candy.
We licked and we licked
and we licked and we licked.

We walked home from the cotton field,
late in the evening,
with the moon shining pretty on the land.